Rumpelstiltskin

and other stories

First published in 2002 by Miles Kelly Publishing,
Bardfield Centre, Great Bardfield, Essex CM7 4SL

24681097531

Copyright © Miles Kelly Publishing Ltd 2002

Project manager: Paula Borton
Editorial Assistant: Nicola Sail

British Library Cataloguing-in-Publication Data
A catalogue record for this book is available from the British Library

ISBN 1-84236-094-9

Printed in Hong Kong

Visit us on the web:
www.mileskelly.net
Info@mileskelly.net

Rumpelstiltskin
and other stories

Chosen by Fiona Waters

MiLes KeLLy PUBLISHING

Contents

Rumpelstiltskin

a retelling from the original tale by the Brothers Grimm

nce upon a time there was a miller. He was a foolish man who was always boasting. Then he went too far.

The king was riding past the mill with his huntsmen one day. The miller's daughter was sitting in the doorway, spinning. The king could not help noticing that she was a very pretty girl so he began talking to her. Her father came bustling up and began to tell the king what a splendid daughter she was.

"Why, your Majesty, she can even spin straw into gold!" boasted the ridiculous miller.

Needless to say, the poor girl could do nothing of the sort but the king thought this was an excellent way to refill the palace treasure house which was rather empty, so he took her back to the palace. He put her in a room with a great pile of straw and told her he wanted to see it all spun into gold the next morning, or else it would be the worse for her.

As soon as the door was locked she began to cry. The task was impossible. Then she heard a thin little voice.

"Do stop crying! You will make the straw all wet, and then we will have no chance of turning it into gold!"

There in front of her stood a strange little man. He had a tiny round body with long skinny legs and huge feet. His clothes looked as if they had seen better days, and on his head he wore a tall battered-looking hat.

"If you give me your necklace, I will do what the king has asked of you," he snapped.

The miller's daughter

unclasped her necklace and handed it to the little man. He
hid it deep in one of his pockets, and sat down by the
spinning wheel. The spinning wheel turned in a blur. The
pile of straw grew smaller, and the mound of shining gold
grew higher. As the first light of day shone in through the
window it was all done. The strange little man disappeared
as suddenly as he had appeared.

The king was delighted with the great pile of gold, and
asked the miller's daughter to marry him. She was too shy
to reply so the king just took her silence as her agreement
and married her anyway that afternoon.

For a while all was well. But then the treasure house
grew empty again so once more the poor girl, now the

queen, was locked in a room with a pile of straw and a spinning wheel.

As the queen wept, once more the strange little man appeared. The queen asked him to help her again, and offered him all the rich jewels she was wearing. But the strange little man was not interested in jewels this time.

"You must promise to give me your first born child," he whispered.

The queen was desperate. But she promised and the little man sat down at the spinning wheel. A great pile of gold appeared by the side of the spinning wheel, and by dawn the straw had all gone. The king was delighted and for a while all was well. Then the queen gave birth to a beautiful baby, and she remembered with dread her promise to the strange little man. Seven days after the baby was born, he appeared by the side of the cradle. The queen wept and wept.

"There you go again," said the little man crossly. "always crying!"

"I will do anything but let you have my baby," cried the queen.

"Very well then, anything to make you stop crying." said the little man, who by now was dripping wet from all the queen's tears. "If you can guess my name in three days, I will let you keep your baby," he said and disappeared as suddenly as he had appeared.

The next morning the little man appeared by the side of the cradle. The queen had sent messengers out far and wide to see if anyone knew the strange little man's name.

"Is it Lacelegs?" she asked.

"No!"

"Is it Wimbleshanks?"

"No!"

"Is it Bandyknees?"

"No!"

and the little man disappeared as suddenly as he had appeared.

The queen sent out even more messengers to the lands far beyond the borders of the kingdom. The second morning the strange little man appeared by the side of the cradle.

"Is it Bluenose?" the queen asked.

"No!"

"Is it Longtooth?"

"No!"

"Is it Skinnyribs?"

"No!" and the little man disappeared with a nasty laugh.

The queen waited up all night as her messengers came in one by one, and just as she was giving up all hope of saving her precious baby, in came the very last one. He was utterly exhausted but he brought the queen the best of news. In a deep, deep, dark forest he had found a strange little man dancing round a fire, singing this song.

> *Today I brew, today I bake,*
> *Tomorrow I will the baby take.*
> *The queen will lose the game,*
> *Rumpelstiltskin is my name!*

The strange little man appeared by the cradle. The queen pretended she still did not know his name.

"Is it Gingerteeth?" she asked.

"No!" said the little man, and he picked the baby up.

"Is is Silverhair?" asked the queen.

"No!" said the little man, and he started to walk towards the door, with a wicked smile.

"Is it Rumpelstiltskin?" asked the queen, and she ran up to the strange little man.

"Some witch told you that!" shrieked the little man, and he stamped his foot so hard that he fell through the floor and was never seen again. The queen told the king the whole story and he was so pleased his baby and his queen were safe that he forgot to be cross with the miller who had told such a terrible fib in the first place!

Liam and the Fairy Cattle

an Irish legend

L iam and his mother lived by the sea. They had a small white cottage with a pile of peat for the fire outside, and a row of potatoes to eat with the fish that Liam would catch. They had two cows, and Liam's mother would make butter and cheese from their milk. She baked bread and gathered sweet heather honey from the hives at the bottom of the meadow. They did not have much in life, but they were happy.

But then there came a time when ill luck fell on the small white cottage. First the two cows died, one after the other, and there was no cheese to eat. Then the shoals of fish swam far out to sea and Liam would come home empty handed. The potatoes rotted in the ground, and Liam and his mother were hungry all the time.

One day when Liam was wandering along the shoreline he came across two boys throwing stones at a seal.

He shouted at the boys and
chased them away, but
when he went to see if
the seal needed help
it turned its head
once and looked
deep into his eyes
then slipped away
into the sea. As it
dived into the waves he
saw blood on its head.

Three days later
when Liam and his
mother were sitting by the
fire in the evening there came
a knock at the door. There on the
doorstep stood an old, old man leaning
on a staff. His clothes looked wet through and he
had a large cut on his forehead, but his eyes were gentle.

"I am very weary, might I come in and warm myself at
your fire?" the old man asked.

Liam opened the door wide, and bid the old man come
in. His mother pulled up a stool close to the fire, and
warmed up the last of the soup in the pot while she bathed
the wound on his head. He thanked her kindly, smiling at
Liam, and Liam had the strangest feeling he had looked
into those deep brown eyes before. But he made up the fire

for the night and they all slept peacefully until the day.

The old man looked better for his night's shelter, and as he rose to leave he spoke to Liam's mother.

"I have no money to offer you but I would like to thank you for your shelter and food, and I would like to repay the boy here for his kindness," and he turned and looked at Liam with his gentle brown eyes. "I know you have lost your cows so I will tell you where you can find some special cows who will give you milk such as you have never tasted before. Tonight is a full moon and the sea-folk will bring their cattle up out of the sea to graze on the lush green grass that grows just beyond the shoreline."

Liam's mother laughed.

"I have often heard tales of these marvellous cattle, but in all the years I have lived here I have never seen a fairy cow."

"That is because your eyes have not been opened by a touch with the heather that grows on the grave of Fionn who died all those years ago," said the old man and there in his hand he held out a sprig of heather. "Will you let me touch your eyes, and the boy's too?

Then you shall see what you shall see."

Well, Liam's mother felt she had nothing to fear from this kindly old man and so both she and Liam let him touch their eyes with the sprig of heather.

"Now," he said, "you must gather seven handfuls of earth from the churchyard, and then tonight go to the meadow just beyond the shoreline. There you will see the fairy cattle. Choose the seven you like the best and throw the earth onto each one. They will all run back to the sea, save the seven that you have chosen. Bring those seven back home and look after them in your kindly way and they will be with you always. Now I must return from whence I came. Liam, will you walk with me to the sea?" and the old man looked at Liam with those gentle eyes once again.

So Liam and the strange old man walked to the shoreline. One moment they were together on the sand, the next Liam was alone. But when he looked out to sea, there was a seal, looking at him with gentle brown eyes. Then with a ripple, it was gone under the waves.

That night, Liam and his mother did as the old man had bid.

They gathered the earth from the churchyard and made
their way quietly down to the meadow. There indeed was
the herd of fairy cattle. They were small, no bigger than a
sheepdog, and all colours, brown and black and white and
brindled. Liam and his mother choose three black, three
white and a brindled one, and Liam crept up behind them
and threw the earth onto their backs. The rest of the herd
scattered back down to the shore and ran
into the waves where they quickly
disappeared. But the seven in the
meadow stood quietly and
showed no fear as Liam and
his mother led them home.

From that day on, Liam
and his mother had
a plentiful supply of rich
creamy milk. The little
fairy cattle would low
gently in the byre and
were well content with
their life on land. But
Liam would never let
them out to graze
when there was a full
moon in case the sea–
folk came to claim
them back.

The North Wind and the Sun

a retelling from Aesop's fables

The North Wind and the Sun once had a quarrel about who was the stronger. "I am stronger than you," said the North Wind. "I can blow down trees, and whip up great waves on the sea."

"I am stronger than you," said the Sun. "I can make flowers open, and turn fields of wheat from green to gold."

And so they argued back and forth, day after day. The East Wind and the Moon became very cross with them both and suggested that they have a competition to decide once and for all who was the strongest. A man was walking down the path, and he was wearing a big overcoat.

"Whichever one of you can first get that man to take off his coat is the strongest," said the Moon. And the East Wind said, "And then we will have no more quarrels!"

So the North Wind and the Sun agreed to the competition. The North Wind began. He blew and blew, the

coldest bitter wind he could manage. The great overcoat
flapped round the man's legs as he struggled against the
wind, but he only pulled the coat closer round his neck to
keep out the bitter cold. Then it was the Sun's turn. She rose
high in the sky and shone down on the man in the great
overcoat. Warmer and warmer she shone, until the man
unbuttoned the coat. Still the Sun beamed
down, and finally the man flung off
the coat, sweat pouring down his
face. The Sun had won!

The North Wind blew off
in a great huff, but he did
not dare continue his quarrel
with the Sun. So today when
the fierce North Wind blows
you have to remember that he
is still very cross!

The Precious Stove

an Austrian folk tale

P eter lived with his mother and father and his
brothers and sisters in an old wooden cottage
deep in the woods of Austria. They were very poor
and the cottage had hardly any
furniture, and they might
have been very cold in
winter were it not for
their most treasured
possession, a stove.
This was no ordinary
stove. It was made of
white porcelain and it
was so tall the gold
crown at the top almost
scraped the ceiling. Its feet
were carved like lion's

claws, the talons painted gold. The sides of the stove were painted with flowers and rare birds, in glowing colours, and the door was tiled in blue and gold. It looked very out of place in the poor wooden cottage for it had originally been made for a king's palace. Many years before, Peter's grandfather had rescued it, after a great war, from the ruins of the palace where he used to work. Peter used to draw copies of the flowers and birds on pieces of brown paper with a stub of old pencil.

One evening, as Peter and his sister Gilda lay curled up in the warmth at the foot of the stove, their father came in, shaking the snow from his boots. He looked tired and ill.

"My children, this is the last night you will be able to enjoy our beautiful stove," he said sadly. "Tomorrow it will be taken away as I have had to sell it. We have no money left, and we need food more than we need a grand stove."

The children were horrified, but their father would not change his mind. That night, instead of banking up the stove to keep it burning warmly through the night, he let the fire die down so it was quite cold in the morning. The traders arrived and loaded the stove onto a cart, and off it rumbled down the track towards the town. Peter's mother and father looked at the handful of gold coins the traders had given them and shook their heads. It seemed a poor bargain when all was said and done.

Peter and Gilda whispered together outside behind the wood pile.

"You have to follow the cart, Peter," said Gilda, "so you can see where our stove goes."

So Peter rushed off down the track after the cart, pausing only to stuff a couple of apples into his pocket. The journey into town was slow as the stove was heavy so the cart could not travel very fast, but by evening it had reached the station. Peter crept as close as he dared, and heard the traders arranging for the stove to go to Vienna by train the very next morning. He made up his mind very quickly. Once the traders had gone to an inn for the night, he clambered up and inside the stove. There was plenty of room inside for a small boy, and he knew that air would come in from the grill at the top under the golden crown. He soon fell fast asleep.

When he awoke, the train was moving fast. It sped through snowy forests and past the mighty Danube river. Peter munched his apples and wondered what his parents would be thinking, and just where was he going to end up, and then what could he do, anyway, to keep the stove for his family.

Eventually the train came to a halt and with much banging and clattering all the boxes around the stove were unloaded onto the platform. Then Peter heard a gruff voice.

"Have a care there! That valuable stove is going to the palace, take care it isn't damaged in any way or it will be the worse for you!"

The palace! Peter's knees shook. The palace, why that was where the king lived. Peter sat as quiet as a mouse as he felt the stove lifted up off the train and onto another cart. It clattered through cobbled streets and over a wooden bridge, and then came to a halt. Many voices came through the grill as the stove was moved off the cart.

"My word, the king will be pleased! Look what a fine stove it is," said one voice.

"It must have come from a palace originally, look at the golden crown at the top," said another.

Then there was silence for a while. Peter strained his ears, and his knees shook a little more. Then he heard the swishing of long robes on a polished floor, and a murmur of voices. Then a deep hush.

"Truly, it is a very beautiful stove. I did not expect it to be so fine. Look at the quality of the painting round the sides," said a deep important voice. And then the handle of the door turned and light flooded into the stove. Peter tumbled out onto the floor as the same deep voice said, "Good gracious! What have we here, there is a child in the stove!"

Peter picked himself up and looked up into eyes that were full of laughter. They belonged to a man dressed in a bright red jacket with great gold tassels and gold buttons. Many glittering medals gleamed on his chest. A great silver sword hung by his side. It was the king!

Peter was absolutely terrified, but the king kept on smiling.

"Well, my boy, would you like to tell me how you come to be inside my new stove?"

A servant rushed forward and grabbed Peter by the arm, meaning to drag him away, but the king raised his hand and the man stepped back.

"Let the child speak," said the king.

Well, once Peter found his tongue, he could not stop. He told the king all about the stove. How it had stood in their poor cottage for as long as he could remember. How much the family welcomed its heat in the winter. And he told the king that his father had been forced to sell the stove for a few gold pieces to buy food.

The king listened in silence while Peter told his story.

"Peter, I am not going to give you back your stove for it belongs here in the palace, but I will give your father several bags of gold, for it is a very valuable stove. And perhaps you would like to stay here and look after it for me?" he asked.

Peter was delighted. And he looked after the stove for the king from that day on. His family never wanted for food again, and every summer they would all come to stay at the palace to see Peter, and the stove of course. When the king discovered how good Peter was at drawing, he sent him to art school and he became a very fine artist. But when he was an old man, all his grandchildren wanted to hear was the story of how he came to Vienna inside a stove!

Amal and the Genie

A Persian fairytale

Many moons ago in ancient Persia there lived a bright young man who knew what was what, and his name was Amal. He was out one day when he had the misfortune to meet a genie. Now sometimes genies can be good news, but this one was in a very bad temper and he was looking for trouble. Amal had to think very quickly. He had no weapons with him, and anyway weapons are no use against genies. All he had in his pocket was an egg and a lump of salt.

The genie came whirling up to Amal, but before he could say anything, Amal yelled at him.

"Genie! You and I should have a competition to see who is the strongest!"

You might think this was very foolish of
Amal, but he knew two things about
genies. One was that it is always
better to take control first, and the
second was that genies are not
terribly bright. They are fine at
conjuring up gorgeous palaces
and flying carpets, but they are a
bit slow when it comes to basic
common sense.

Well, the genie looked at
Amal, and then he laughed and
laughed. It was not a nice sound,
but Amal was not daunted.

"Hah! You don't look very strong," sniggered the genie.
"I shall win this contest easily," and he laughed again.

Amal picked up a stone.

"You must squeeze this stone until water comes out of
it," he said, handing the genie the stone.

Well, the genie squeezed and squeezed, and huffed and
puffed, but, of course, no water came out of the stone. He
threw it down in a temper.

"Not possible!" he snapped.

Amal bent down and picked up the stone, and
squeezed. And with a scrunching sound, liquid ran down
Amal's fingers.

The genie was astonished. And so would you have been if

you had been there. What clever Amal had done was to put the egg in the same hand as the stone, and it was the egg that was broken. But as I said, genies are not terribly bright and this one was no exception. Then Amal said, "Well, I win

that one. But now perhaps you could crumble this stone into powder," and he handed the genie another stone.

Well, the genie squeezed and squeezed, and huffed and puffed, but, of course, the stone did not crumble at all, not even the tiniest bit. The genie threw it down in a temper.

Amal picked it up and squeezed. And as he squeezed, powder fell from his fingers with a grinding sound. The genie was astonished. And so would you have been if you had been there, but you can guess what clever Amal had done. He put the salt in his hand as well as the stone.

The genie was feeling that his reputation was somewhat dented by Amal's performance so he needed to get his own back.

"You are clearly a great and mighty fighter," the genie said to Amal. "I should like to give you a meal to celebrate your achievements. Come and stay the night with me," and he smiled.

But Amal saw the smile, and kept his wits about him. After a dreadful meal (the genie was not a very good cook either) they both lay down to sleep in the genie's cave. Once Amal was sure the genie was asleep, he moved to the other side of the cave, leaving his pillow in the bed to look as if he were still there asleep. Then he watched. As the first light

of dawn filtered into the cave, the genie woke up. He picked up a huge club and crept over to where he thought Amal was lying, and he pounded the club down onto the bed, seven times in all. Then he stomped out of the cave to fetch some water for his morning tea.

You can imagine his utter dismay when, on returning, he found Amal singing to himself as he lit the fire.

"Good morning, genie! I thought I would get breakfast ready," said Amal cheerfully. "I hope you slept better than I did," he continued. "Some wretched insect batted me in the face in the night, seven times in all."

Well, at this the genie gave a great shriek and whistled himself as fast as possible into an old oil lamp that lay on the floor of the cave. He wasn't seen again for hundreds and hundreds of years until a young lad called Aladdin happened to find the lamp. But that is another story, isn't it?

The Princess and the Pea

a retelling from the original story by Hans Christian Andersen

The prince was very fed up. Everyone in the court, from his father, the king, down to the smallest page, seemed to think it was time he was married. Now the prince would have been very happy to get married, but he did insist that his bride be a princess, a real true and proper princess. He had travelled the land and met plenty of nice girls who said they were princesses, but none, it seemed to him, were really true and proper princesses. Either their manners were not quite exquisite enough, or their feet were much too big. So he sat in the palace, reading dusty old history books and getting very glum.

One night, there was the most terrible storm. Rain was lashing down, and thunder and lightning rolled and flashed round the palace. The wind kept blowing out the candles, and everyone huddled closer to the fire. Suddenly there was a great peal from the huge front door bell.

And there, absolutely dripping wet, stood a princess. Well, she said she was a princess, but never did anyone look less like a princess. Her hair was plastered to her head, her dress was wringing wet and her silk shoes were covered in mud. She was quite alone, without even the smallest maid, and just where had she come from? But she kept insisting she was a princess.

We will see about that, thought the queen. While the dripping girl sat sipping a mug of warm milk and honey, the queen went to supervise the making of the bed in the second-best spare bedroom. She didn't think it necessary to put their late night visitor in the best spare bedroom, after all she might only be a common-or-garden duchess. The queen told the maids to take all the bedclothes and the mattress off the bed. Then she placed one single pea right on the middle of the bedstead. Next the maids piled twenty mattresses on top of the pea, and then twenty feather quilts on top of the mattresses. And thus the girl was left for the night.

In the morning, the queen swept into the bedroom in her dressing gown and asked the girl how she had slept.

"I didn't sleep a wink all night." said the girl. "There was a great, hard lump in the middle of the bed. It was quite dreadful. I am sure I am black and blue all over!"

Now everyone knew she really must be a princess, for only a real princess could be as soft-skinned as that. The prince was delighted, and insisted they got married at once, and they lived very happily ever after. They always slept in very soft beds, and the pea was placed in the museum, where it probably still is today.

Why the Manx Cat
has no Tail

a myth from the Isle of Man

The rain was falling in torrents, and there were great storm clouds building up. The rivers were overflowing and the fields looked like lakes. Noah decided that the time had come to fill his ark as planned with two of every animal that lived. He called his sons Shem and Ham and Japeth and they began rounding up the animals and leading them gently onto the ark.

First came the big beasts, the giraffes and lions and elephants. Then came the cows and the sheep and the pigs. Then came the foxes and the rabbits, but not together of course. Then came the birds and the grasshoppers and the ants, who were rather nervous of the elephants' feet. Finally came the dogs, but only one cat, a big ginger tom cat. The she-cat, who was a stripy tabby, had decided that she would like to go mousing one last time, as she realised she would not be able to eat a fellow passenger when they were all cooped up in the ark.

Mrs Noah called and called her, but still she did not come. Cats are always contrary and she was no exception. Noah looked at the rising water and told Mrs Noah that he would have to pull up the gangplank as the ark would soon be afloat. All the other animals were settling in to their various stalls, and what a noise there was! Roaring and mooing, trumpeting and baaing, snorting and squawking. Toes and flippers and

trotters and paws got stood on, fur and feathers were ruffled
and horns and long tails got stuck, but eventually everyone
was in place.

Noah began to pull the great door of the ark to, and
just as he was about to shut it fast, up pranced the she-cat,
soaking wet but licking her lips. She managed to slip
through the gap in the nick of time but her great plume of
a tail was caught in the door as it slammed shut. She turned
round and her entire tail was cut off! The cat was very

cross, but Noah told her it was entirely her own fault and she would have to wait until they found land again before she could have her tail mended.

Forty days and forty nights later, the flood was over and Noah opened the great door of the ark once more. First out was the she-cat, and she ran and ran until she found the Isle of Man, and there she stopped, too ashamed for anyone else to see her. Ever since then the cats from the Isle of Man have had no tails. Nowadays they are rather proud to be different.

Jack and the Beanstalk

a retelling from the original tale by Joseph Jacobs

This is the story of how Jack did a silly thing, but all was well in the end.

Jack and his mother were very poor and there came a sad day when there was just no more money left, so Jack's mother told him to take the cow to market and sell her.

As Jack led the cow to market, he met a funny little man with a tall feather in his hat.

"And where might you be going with that fine-looking cow?" the funny little man asked.

Jack explained and the funny little man swept off his hat with the tall feather, and shook out five coloured beans.

"Well, young Jack, I can save you a journey. I will give

you these five magic beans in exchange for your cow."

Now Jack should have realised that this was all rather odd, for how did the funny little man know his name? But once he heard the word "magic" he didn't stop to think. He took the beans at once, gave the funny little man the cow and ran off home to his mother.

"Jack, you are a complete fool! You have exchanged our fine cow for five worthless beans!" She flung the beans out of the window, and sent Jack to bed without any supper.

When he woke in the morning, Jack couldn't understand why it was so dark in the cottage. He rushed outside to find his mother staring in amazement at the most enormous beanstalk that reached right up into the clouds.

"I told you they were magic beans," smiled Jack, and without any hesitation he began to climb the beanstalk. He climbed and climbed until he could no longer see the ground below. When he reached the top there stood a vast castle. Jack knocked at the door, and it was opened by a HUGE woman!

"My husband eats little boys for breakfast so you better run away quickly," she said to Jack. But before Jack could reply, the ground started to shake and tremble.

"Too late!" said the giant's wife. "You must hide," and she bundled Jack into a cupboard. Jack peeped through the keyhole, and saw the most colossal man stump into the kitchen.

"Fee fi fo fum! I smell the blood of an Englishman!" he roared.

"Don't be silly, dear. You can smell the sausages I have just cooked for your breakfast," said the giant's wife, placing a plate piled high with one hundred and sixty-three sausages in front of him. The giant did not seem to have very good table manners, and had soon gobbled the lot. Then he poured a great bag of gold onto the table, and counted all the coins.

With a smile on his big face, he soon fell asleep.

Jack darted out of the cupboard, grabbed the bag of money and hared out of the kitchen. He slithered down the beanstalk as fast as ever he could and there, still standing at the bottom, was his mother. She was astonished when she saw the gold.

Jack's mother bought two new cows and she and Jack were very content now they had plenty to eat every day. But after a while Jack decided he would like to climb the beanstalk again. The giant's wife was not very pleased to see him.

"My husband lost a bag of gold the last time you were here," she muttered looking closely at Jack, but then the ground began to shake and tremble. Jack hid in the cupboard again.

The giant stumped into the kitchen.

"Fee fi fo fum! I smell the blood of an Englishman!" he roared.

"Don't be silly, dear. You can smell

the chickens I have just cooked for your breakfast," said the giant's wife, placing a plate piled high with thirty-eight chickens in front of him. The giant had soon gobbled the lot. Then he lifted a golden hen onto the table, and said, "Lay!" and the hen laid a golden egg. With a smile on his big face he fell asleep, snoring loudly.

Jack darted out of the cupboard, grabbed the golden hen and hared out of the kitchen. He slithered down the beanstalk as fast as ever he could and there, still standing at the bottom, was his mother. She was astonished when she saw the hen.

Jack's mother bought a whole herd of cows and found a farmer to look after them. She bought lots of new clothes for herself and Jack, and they were very content. But after a while Jack decided he would like to climb the beanstalk one last time. The giant's wife was not at all pleased to see him.

"My husband lost a golden hen the last time you were here," and she peered closely at Jack, but then the ground began to shake and tremble. This time Jack hid under the table.

The giant stumped into the kitchen.

"Fee fi fo fum! I smell the blood of an Englishman!" he roared.

"I would look in the cupboard if I were you," said the giant's wife, but of course the cupboard was empty. They were both puzzled. The giant trusted his nose, and his wife didn't know where Jack had gone.

"Eat your breakfast, dear. I have just cooked you ninety-two fried eggs," said the giant's wife, placing a plate in front of him. The giant had soon gobbled the lot. Then he lifted a golden harp onto the table, and said, "Play!" and the harp played so sweetly that the giant was soon fast asleep, snoring loudly.

Jack crept out from under the table and grabbed the golden harp, but as soon as he touched it the harp called out, "Master, master!" and the giant awoke with a great start. He chased after Jack who scrambled down the beanstalk as fast as ever he could with the harp in his arms. As soon as Jack reached the ground he raced to get a big axe and chopped through the beanstalk. Down tumbled the great beanstalk, down tumbled the giant and that was the end of them both!

Jack and his mother lived very happily for the rest of their days. The bag of gold never ran out, the hen laid a golden egg every day, and the harp soon forgot about the giant and played sweetly for Jack and his mother.

The Gingerbread Boy

an English folk tale

One fine sunny day, an old woman was making some ginger biscuits. She had a little dough left over and so she made a gingerbread boy. She gave him two raisins for eyes and three cherries for buttons, and put a smile on his face with a piece of orange peel. And she popped him in the oven. But as she lifted the tray out of the oven when the biscuits were cooked, the gingerbread boy hopped off the tray and ran straight out of the door! The old woman ran after him, and her husband ran after her, but they couldn't catch the gingerbread boy. He called out, "Run, run, as fast as you can! You can't catch me, I'm the gingerbread man!"

The old dog in his kennel ran after the old man and the old woman, but he couldn't catch the

gingerbread boy. The ginger cat, who had been asleep in
the sun, ran after the dog, but she couldn't catch the
gingerbread boy. He called out,

"Run, run, as fast as you can! You can't catch me, I'm
the gingerbread man!"

The brown cow in the meadow lumbered after the cat,
but she couldn't catch the gingerbread boy. The black horse
in the stable galloped after the cow but he couldn't catch
the gingerbread boy. He called out,

"Run, run, as fast as you can! You can't catch me,
I'm the gingerbread man!"

The fat pink pig in the sty trotted after the horse, but
she couldn't catch the gingerbread boy. The rooster flapped
and squawked after the pig but he couldn't catch the
gingerbread boy. He called out,

"Run, run, as fast as you can! You can't catch me,
I'm the gingerbread man!"

He ran and ran, and the old woman and the old
man, the dog and the cat, the cow and the horse, the
pig and the rooster all ran after him. He kept on
running until he came to the river. For the first time
since he had hopped out of the oven, the
gingerbread boy had
to stop running.

"Help, help! How
can I cross the
river?" he cried.

47

A sly fox suddenly appeared by his side.

"I could carry you across," said the sly fox.

The gingerbread boy jumped onto the fox's back, and the fox slid into the water.

"My feet are getting wet," complained the gingerbread boy.

"Well, jump onto my head," smiled the fox, showing a lot of very sharp teeth. And he kept on swimming.

"My feet are still getting wet," complained the gingerbread boy again after a while. "Well, jump onto my nose," smiled the fox, showing even more very sharp teeth.

The gingerbread boy jumped onto the fox's nose, and SNAP! the fox gobbled him all up. When the fox climbed out of the river on the other side, all that was left of the naughty gingerbread boy was a few crumbs. So the old woman and the old man, the dog and the cat, the cow and the horse, the pig and the rooster all went home and shared the ginger biscuits. They were delicious.